Balzer + Bray
An Imprint of HarperCollinsPublishers

little butterfly

LAURA LOGAN

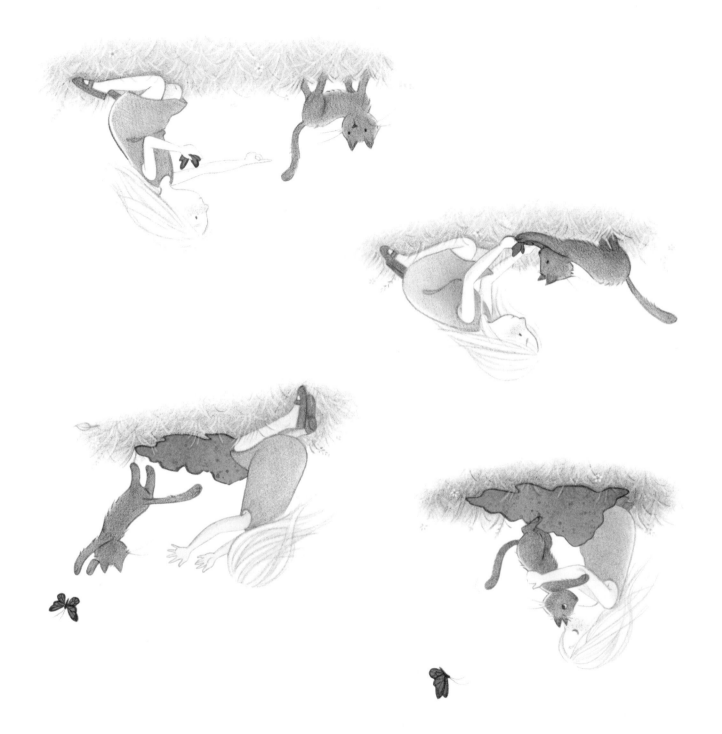

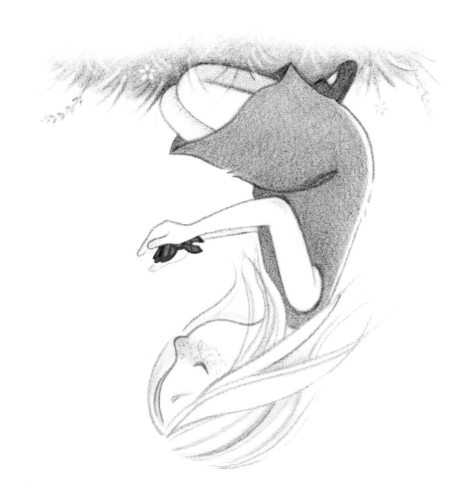

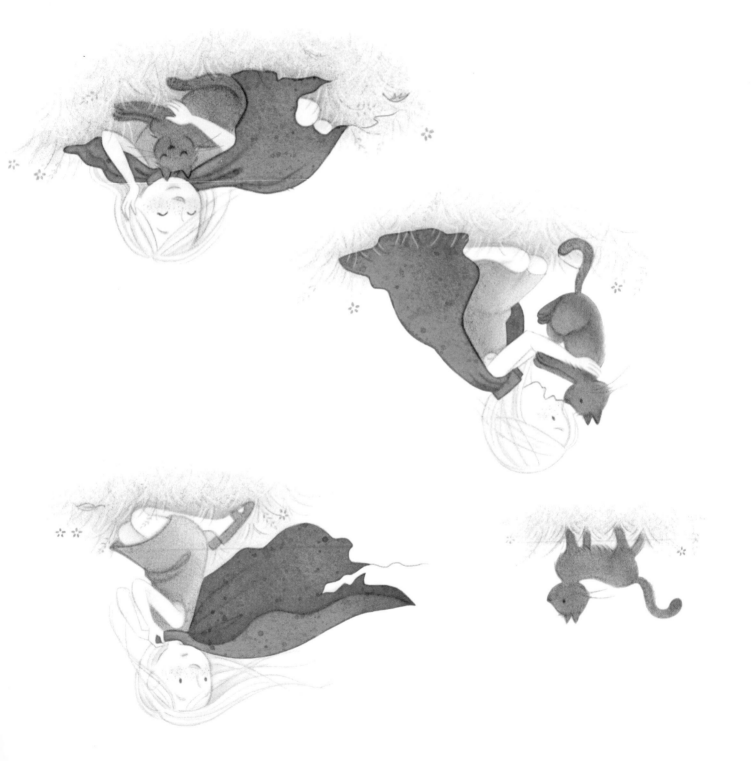

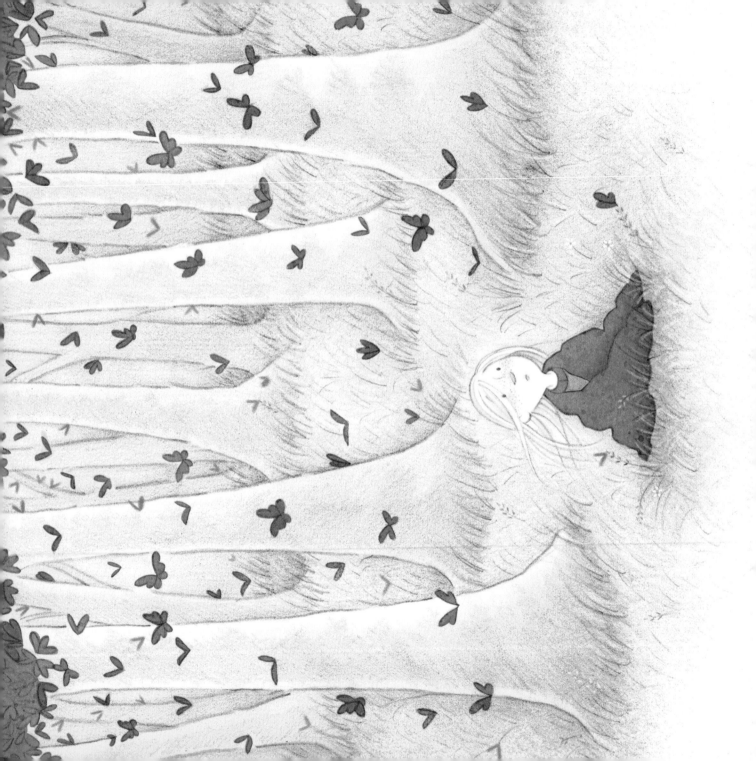

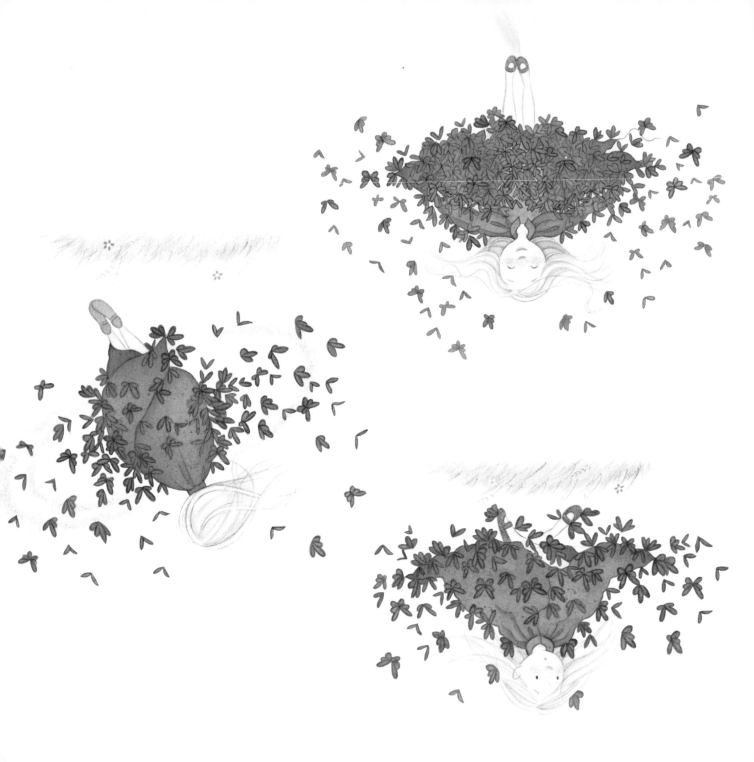

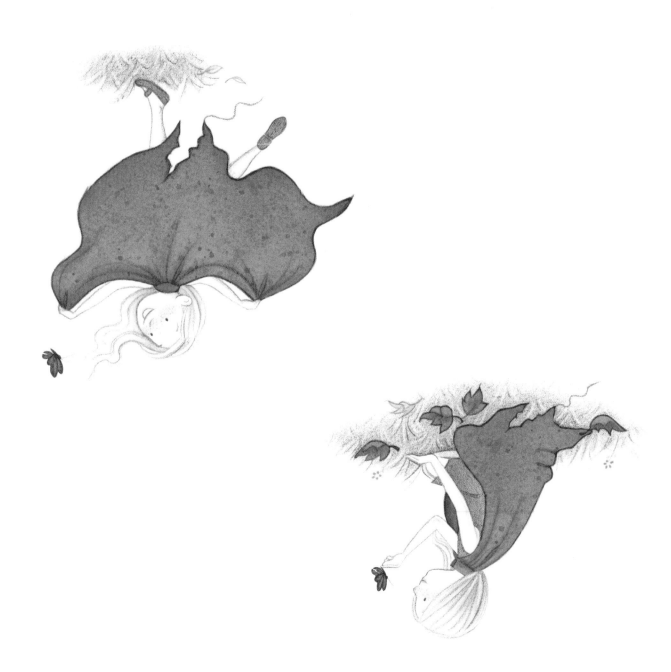

author's note

Monarch butterflies have always held a special place in my heart. Seeing one would stop me in my tracks when I was a child. Against the backdrop of a bright-blue Texas sky, their beautiful orange-and-black markings looked to me like stained-glass windows illuminated by the sun. I would stare until I could no longer make out the flutter of those glowing wings. I thought if I looked long enough, I could burn that image into my mind and never lose it.

For me, no creature symbolizes growth and change like a butterfly. My children and I have raised monarch caterpillars and witnessed their truly exciting metamorphoses firsthand. But what monarchs do every fourth generation is even more astonishing: The butterflies embark on a daunting migratory journey across North America. Depending on where in the country they originate, monarchs can fly up to 2,500 miles to spend their winters in central Mexico. Their resilience in migrating such long distances is awe-inspiring. How do they know where to go? They've never been there before.

The little girl in this story offers kindness to the injured butterfly. Her heartfelt gesture toward the smallest of creatures has the power to alter the butterfly's course—and her own. This "butterfly effect," whether real or the stuff of her dreams, is transformative. Her kindness is returned and comes back to her in abundance—as a joyful, fantastical journey, on the gentle wings of butterflies.

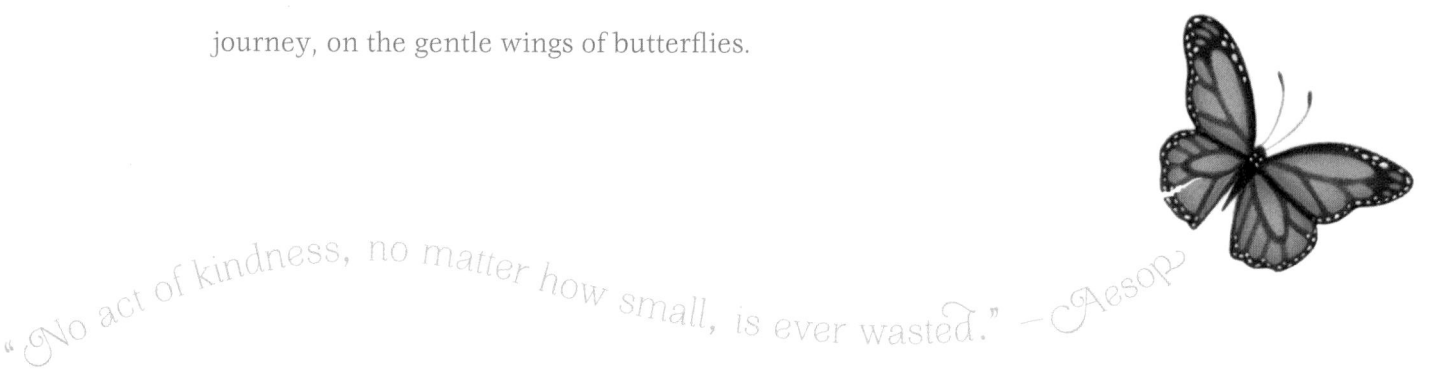

"No act of kindness, no matter how small, is ever wasted." —Aesop

For Brian, Henry, and Josephine, with all my love

Balzer + Bray is an imprint of HarperCollins Publishers.

Little Butterfly

www.harpercollinschildrens.com

Library of Congress Control Number: 2014958704
ISBN 978-0-06-228126-5 (trade bdg.)

The artist used pencil, Corel Painter, and Adobe Photoshop
to create the digital illustrations for this book.
Typography by Ellice M. Lee
15 16 17 18 19   SCP   10 9 8 7 6 5 4 3 2 1
❖
First Edition